TALE OF
THE GOOD RAT

WRITTEN BY MIKE JOENS
ILLUSTRATED BY LEN SIMON

A Whitestone Media Little Overhill Book™

COVER DESIGN AND LAYOUT BY SHANNONRENEE.COM
THEO COTTAGE ILLUSTRATION BY MIKE HODGSON

FIRST EDITION PRINTED IN U.S.A. BY WORZALLA, JULY 2013

ISBN: 9789751312433

FROM MIKE TO DAKODA AND AIDEN
FROM LEN TO CHARLIE AND COOPER

WWW.THEOPRESENTS.COM

ONCE THERE WAS A YOUNG SHREW named
Simon who lived in a snug burrow along the
banks of the River Coln. It was Saturday morning,
which meant it was market day in the nearby village
of Little Overhill. Simon loved going to market to
purchase goodies such as beetles and spiders and
worms and snails to bake in his pies.
Woodlice and grub pies were
his very favorite!

Simon put on his favorite green vest with gold trim. He combed his hair and brushed his teeth, for he wanted to look especially well-groomed while shopping in the village. He even cleaned his fingernails, which took some doing, because everyone knows that shrews love digging in dirt and mud and that their nails are a frightful mess.

Simon inspected himself in the mirror. Then he got his money purse, put it inside his vest and left his burrow.

It was a cold, windy autumn day,
a perfect day for walking, and as he
made his way along the path that
led to the village he
whistled
a happy
tune.

But as Simon approached the village,
something very dreadful happened.

A gang of weasels leaped out from behind a hedge and attacked him!

They beat him and stripped him of his little green vest with the gold trim, took his money purse, and left him half dead.

Weasels are like that. They have nasty tempers.

Meanwhile, Luther and Belfry, two church mice who lived in Theo's cottage by the river, were on their way to the local rugby field in the village of Little Overhill. There was a big game today.

When they saw Simon lying on the path, beaten up and miserable looking, they shook their heads. "What a dreadful sight," Belfry said. "Who could have done such a thing?"

Luther replied, "Weasels, most likely. Nasty tempers."

Belfry, being a good little church mouse, wished to stop and help. Theo had taught them to be kind to their neighbors, and Belfry knew it was the right thing to do. But Luther was in a hurry to get to the game. They were a bit late, you see, and it wouldn't do to be late to a big game.

"Someone will be along soon, Belfry. You'll see."

"Are you sure?" Belfry asked, with a worried wrinkle in his nose. He knew very well that helping Simon the shrew was much more important than playing rugby, and he felt a little guilty about it. Still, he ran with the ball a little way and then tossed it back to Luther.

"Are you really sure?"

Luther raced
ahead of Belfry.
"Of course I'm sure.
This is a well-traveled path.
Especially on market day."

Belfry felt a little less guilty. "Well, if you say so."

And with that Simon the shrew
was forgotten and the two church
mice practiced rugby plays
all the way to the
village.

And someone *did* come along soon, just as Luther had said.

Miss Matilda Buckthorne was a wee round hedgehog who lived in a hedge of laurel, not far from Theo's cottage. She spent most of her time knitting quilts
and shawls
and potholders
and doilies
for her friends and neighbors.

Hedgehogs are excellent knitters, you see, with an ample supply of knitting needles and a wonderful sense of design. She was on her way to the village to sell her goods.

When she saw Simon lying in the path she let out a startled gasp. "Dear, dear, whatever happened to you?"

Simon let out a mournful groan.

Miss Matilda felt a prickle of fear in her quills. There had been reports of weasels in the area, and everyone knows what nasty tempers they have.

Immediately she curled into a ball, so that she re-
sembled a roly-poly pin cushion. Hedgehogs do that
when they are frightened, you see. She opened one eye
and peeked through her quills for signs of danger—
especially in the dark woods beyond the path. Seeing
no sign of weasels, Miss Matilda uncurled herself
with a snort.

Just then a cold wind blew. Miss Matilda looked down at Simon's poor, shivering body. A single tear trickled down from one of his sad swollen eyes.

"It *is* frightfully chilly, I'm sure," Miss Matilda said, adjusting a knitted scarf around her neck. "I'd give you one of my quilts to cover yourself, but it took me ever so long to knit them. And besides," she added, darting a nervous glance at the woods, "I'm really much too busy to stop at the moment. I must get my goods to market."

So she patted poor Simon's head and smiled. "Not to worry, someone should be along any moment to help you."

Confident she had encouraged poor Simon with her kind words, Miss Matilda scampered down the path with her basket of quilts and shawls.

And wouldn't you know, someone *did* come along the path!

It was none other than Wigglesworth the rat.

Now most of the animals in the village of Little Overhill have no dealings with rats, because rats are—well, *rats*. Rats are messy. They have the most beastly table manners. And if this were not horrible enough, everyone knows that rats carry...*fleas*!

Despite his shabby appearance, Wigglesworth was once the head butler in Nigel Beaver's large house on the river. He was well-educated and quite elegant, as rats go. However, when Nigel Beaver no longer needed his services, Wigglesworth fell on hard times and was in need of a new position. In fact, he was on his way to an interview at Periwinkle Badger's home when he saw Simon lying in the middle of the path.

"I say, Old Bean," Wigglesworth exclaimed in a very grand tone. "Up with you now. It's not healthy to sleep in the middle of the path. Someone might run you over."

But Simon did not get up, nor did he move. He just lay there, shivering.

Wigglesworth's whiskers twitched two times. His whiskers often twitched when things weren't quite right. And things were not quite right.

He looked Simon over with a curious squint. "I say, my good fellow, any idea who did this dreadful thing to you?"

Simon let out a pitiful moan.

The autumn wind blew a little colder.

Wigglesworth frowned. His whiskers began to twitch fiercely.

"This looks like the work of weasels. What terrible tempers they have."

Now Wigglesworth knew that if he stopped to help Simon he would be late for his interview with Periwinkle Badger and might lose his position. Badgers, you see, are quite punctual.

Still he took pity on the shrew. "I must help this poor chap," he said. "I must tend to his wounds. I should never forgive myself if I didn't."

And so he went straightway to work. He washed Simon's wounds as best he could. Then he made a dressing of crushed berries and moss, and placed it on Simon's wounded head.

Simon opened his eyes, managed a weak smile and shivered.

Wigglesworth immediately took off his scarf and coat and wrapped Simon in them tenderly. "How's that, Old Bean?"

The coat was much too big for Simon and there were holes in it, but it was warm, and Simon closed his eyes with a contented smile.

Then Wigglesworth lifted Simon and carried him to Theo's cottage, which was just over the hill. He knew that Theo was a kind man who loved God and loved God's creatures as well. "Theo will take good care of you, you'll see."

Theo was in his garden raking leaves when he saw Wigglesworth carrying Simon the shrew in his arms. "Oh dear, what have we here?" he exclaimed.

"This poor chap's been badly hurt, Theo," Wigglesworth said. "Could you please help?"

"Of course I'll help." Theo took Simon and started at once for his cottage. "Let me take him inside and make him comfortable by the fire. I'll brew some herb broth and we'll fix him right as rain."

Wigglesworth smiled. "Jolly good."

He stayed with Theo until he was certain that Simon would recover. Then he turned to leave, and said, "If there's anything more I can do for him, Theo, please ask for me at Periwinkle Badger's house. I do hope to have a position there, if he will have me. I'm ever so late for my interview."

"I will pray that God gives you favor," Theo said. "Good day!"

Wigglesworth tipped his bowler hat. "Cheerio!" And with a wink and a smile he turned and hurried on his way, feeling wonderfully warm inside.

Now which of these three was a good neighbor
to poor Simon the shrew?

Was it Luther and Belfry,
the two rugby playing church mice?

Was it Miss Matilda Buckthorne,
the knitting hedgehog?